Timeless Tales

My Not-So Small Book of Stories

OFFSHOOT KIDS

CONTENTS

Lalu and Peelu

Mother Hen lived on a farm.

She had two chicks, Lalu and Peelu.

Lalu was red. He loved red things. Peelu was yellow.
He loved yellow things.

One day, Lalu saw something on a plant. It was something red.
He ate it up.

Oh no! It was a red chili. It was too hot. Lalu's mouth burned.
He screamed.

Mother Hen came running. Peelu came too.
Peelu said, "I will get something for you!"

Peelu brought a yellow candy.

Lalu gobbled up the candy. His mouth did not burn anymore.

Mother Hen and Lalu kissed Peelu.

Circle

One day, Rhea sat with her grandmother. Grandmother drew a circle.

"Can you draw one too, Rhea?" Grandmother asked. "Yes, I can," said Rhea. Soon, Rhea drew a circle.

"Now, I will draw a ball," said Grandmother. Grandmother drew three lines on the circle. The circle looked like a ball.

Rhea drew four lines on her circle. The circle looked like a ball.

“Now, let us draw a balloon,” said Grandmother. She added a curved line to the ball.

“The ball looks like a balloon!” Rhea clapped with joy.

Rhea drew many circles. Big and small circles, red, blue, green and yellow circles. She also added curved lines to these circles. And then, there were many balloons.

"Can you draw something else with a circle?" asked Grandmother.

"Yes," said Rhea.

Rhea drew many things with a circle. First, she drew a Sun.

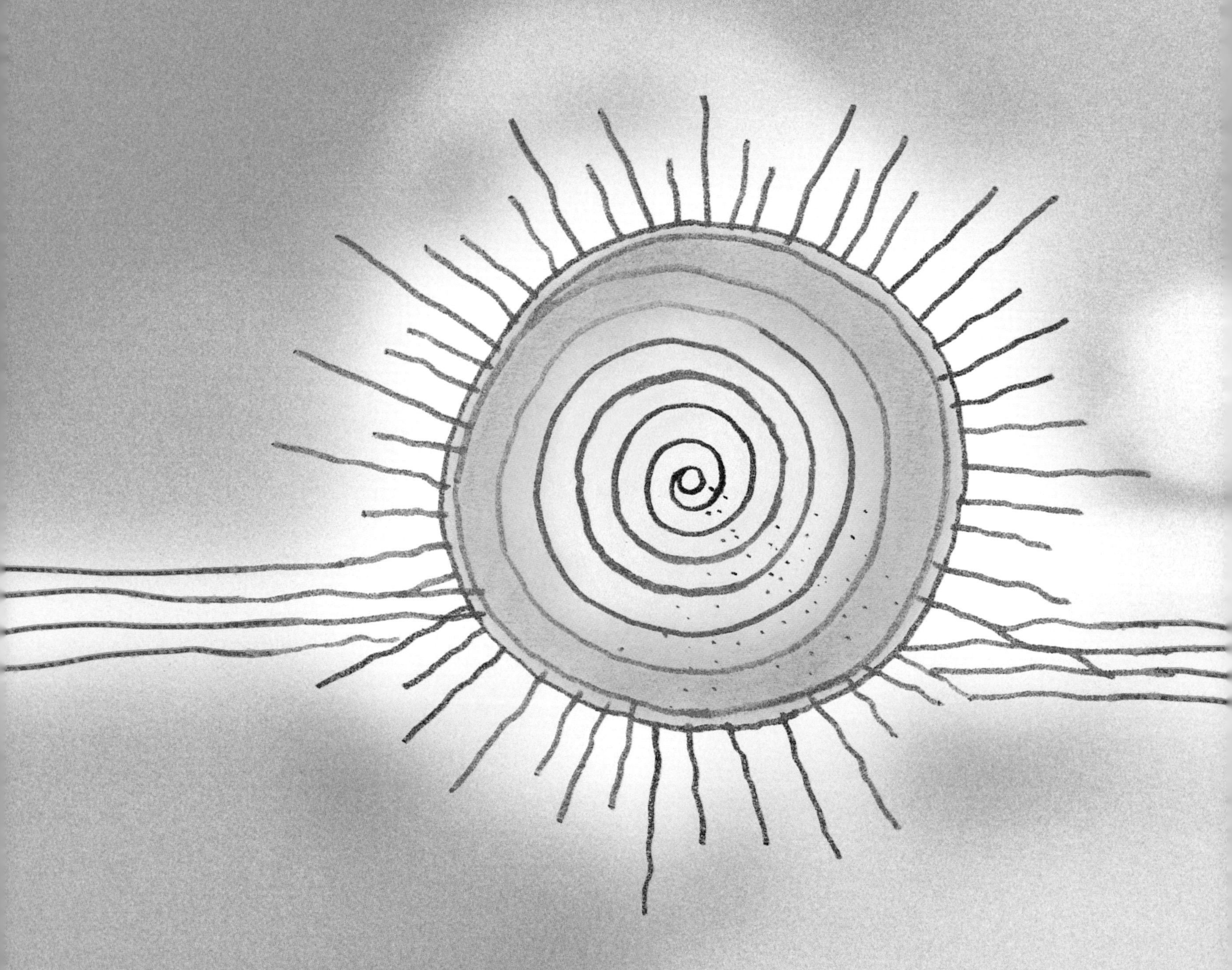

Then she drew a Moon.

Rhea drew a wheel.

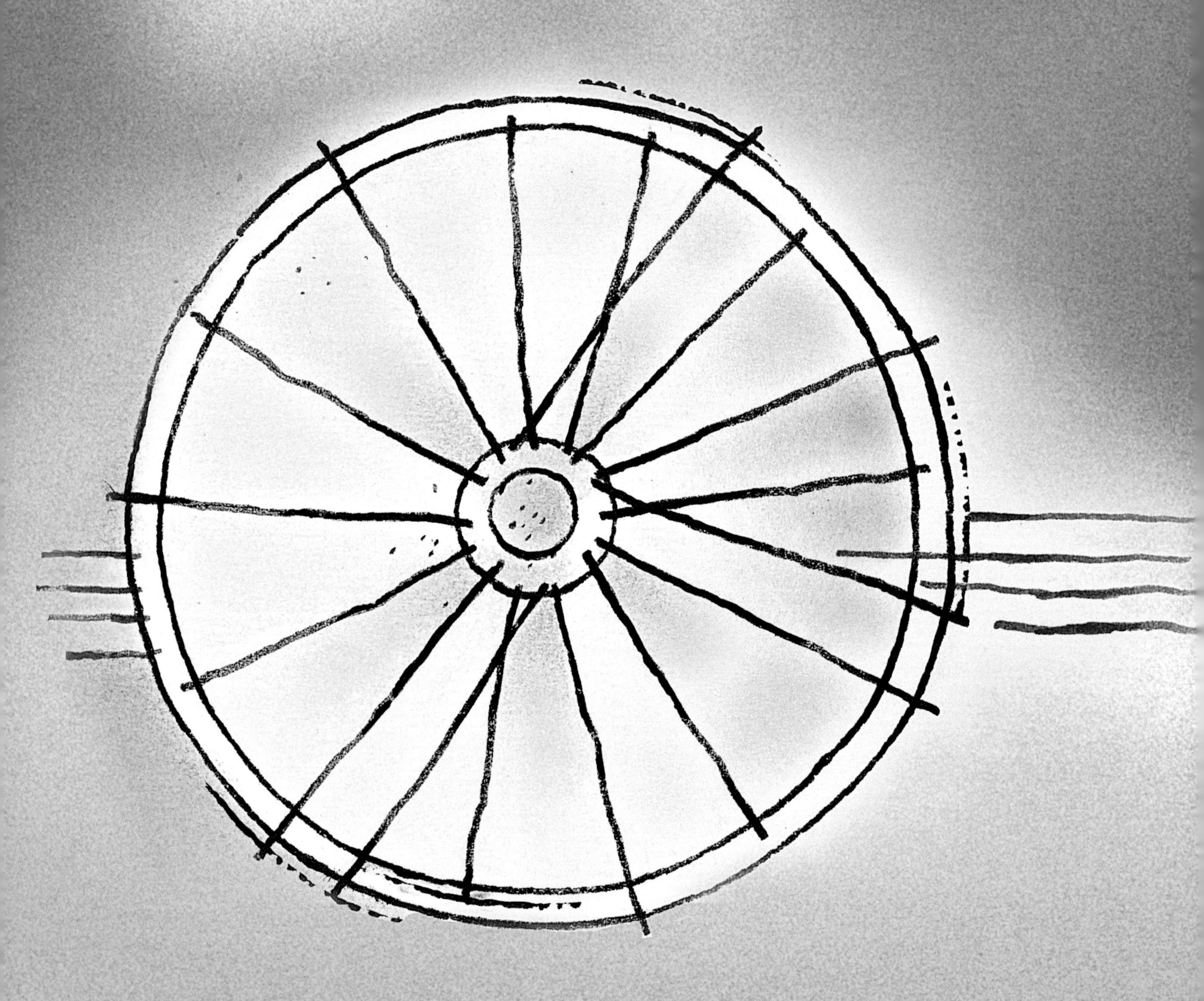

She drew a rabbit too.

Rhea drew many circles. It turned out to be a caterpillar.

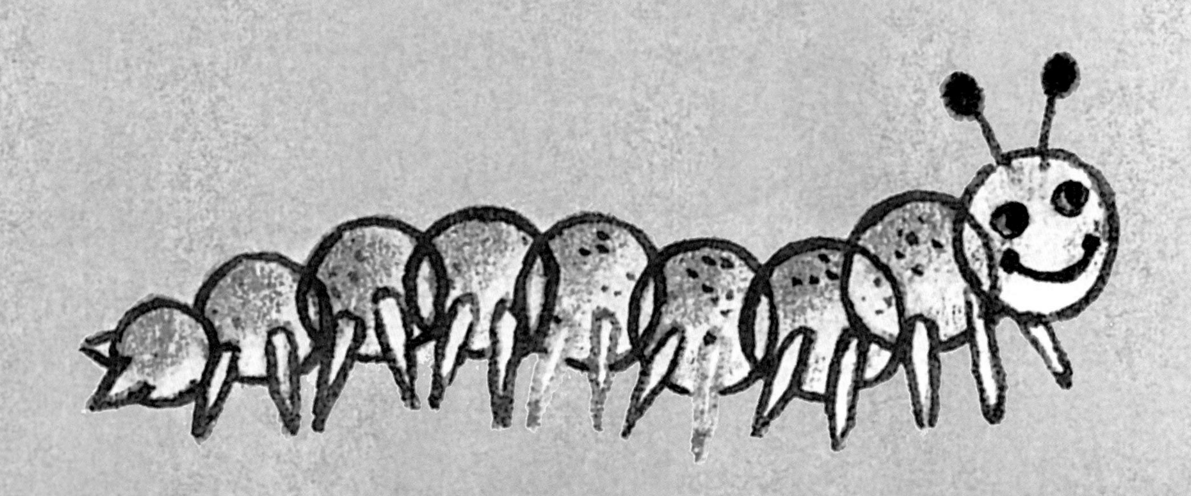

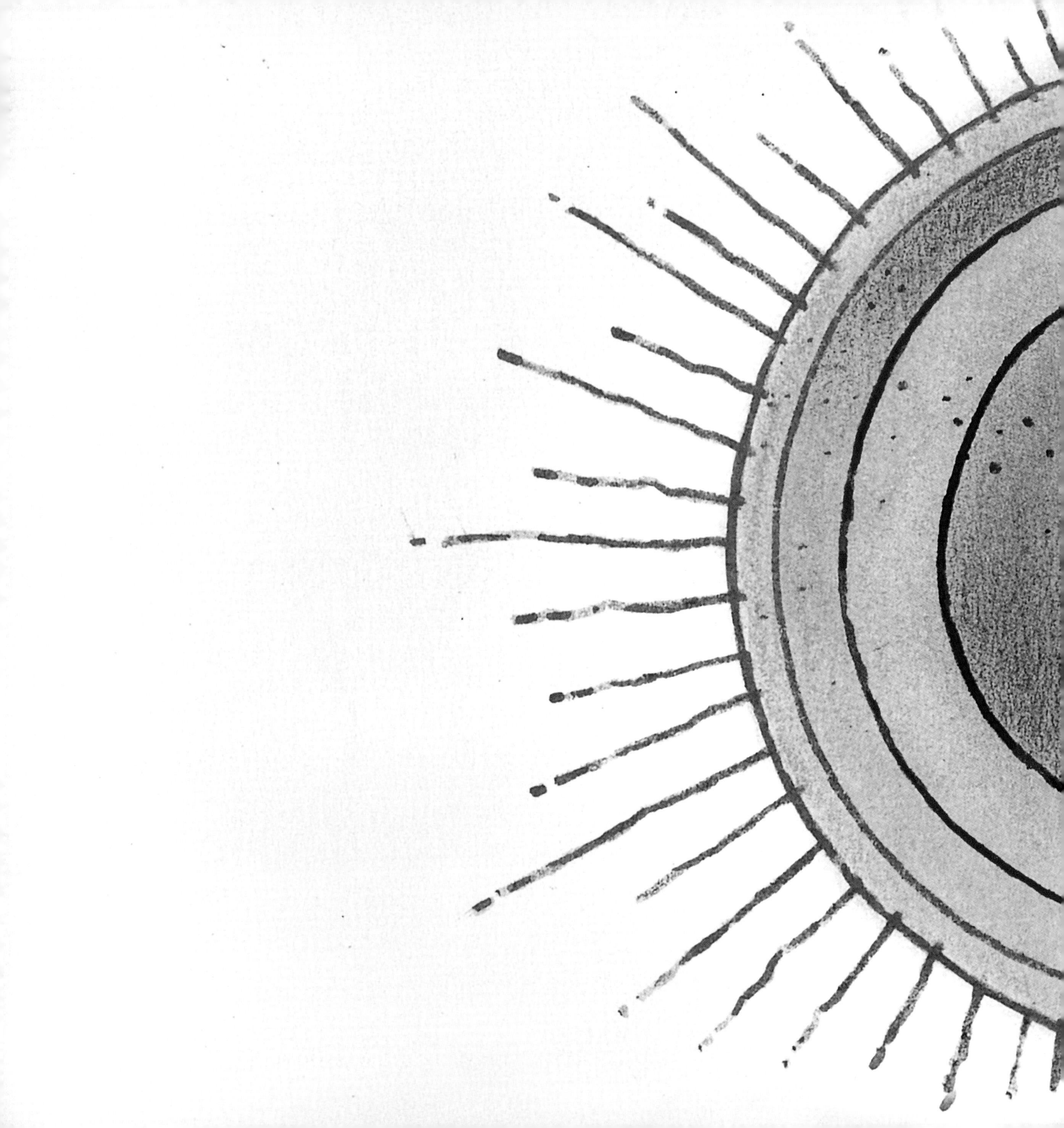

And then, Rhea drew her own face.

THE TABLE

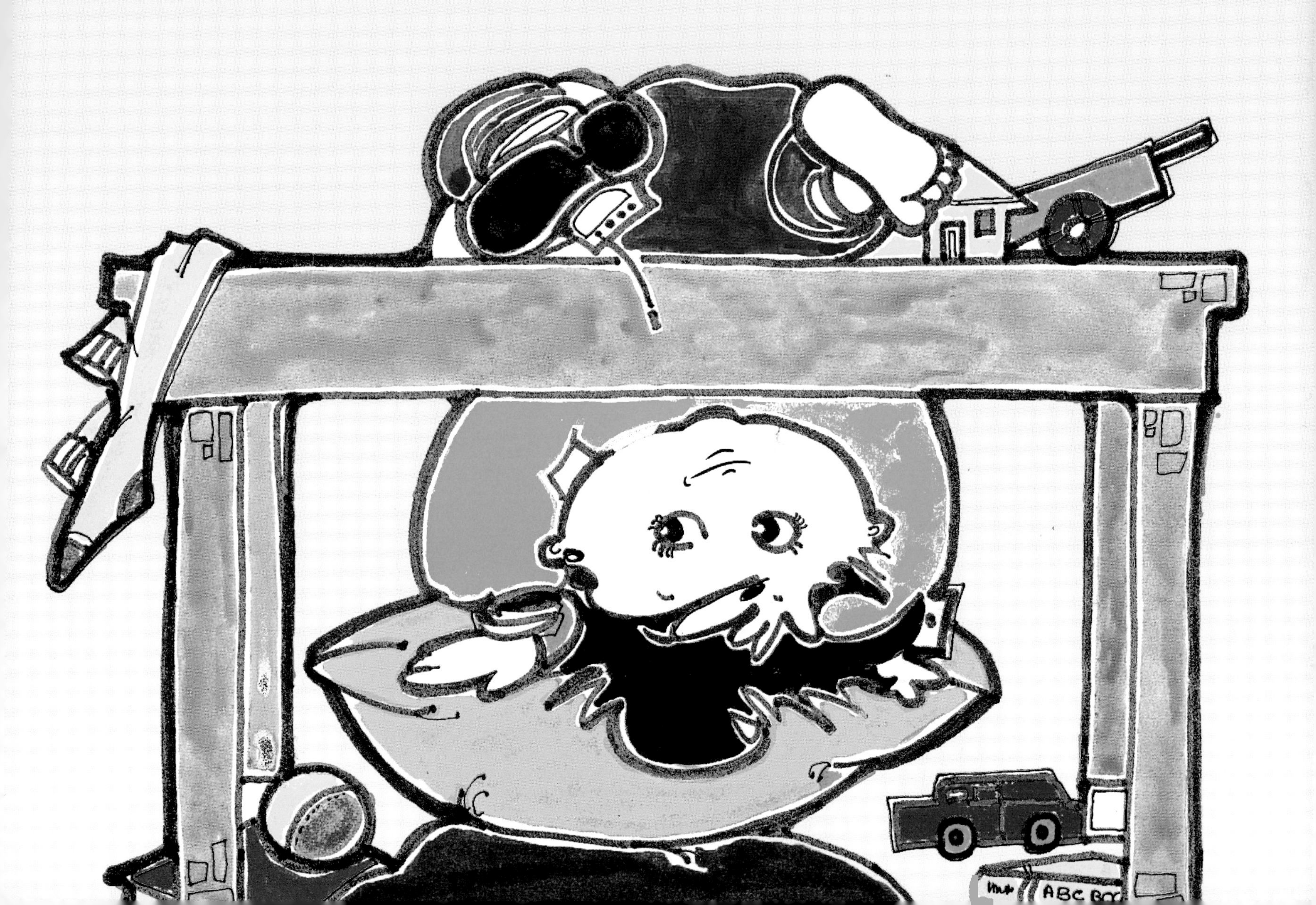

There was a little boy. His name was Neil.

Neil had a table. He liked his table very much. He often used it for fun.

Neil sat on the table and drove his car.

"Beep...beep...beep!" Neil blew the horn.

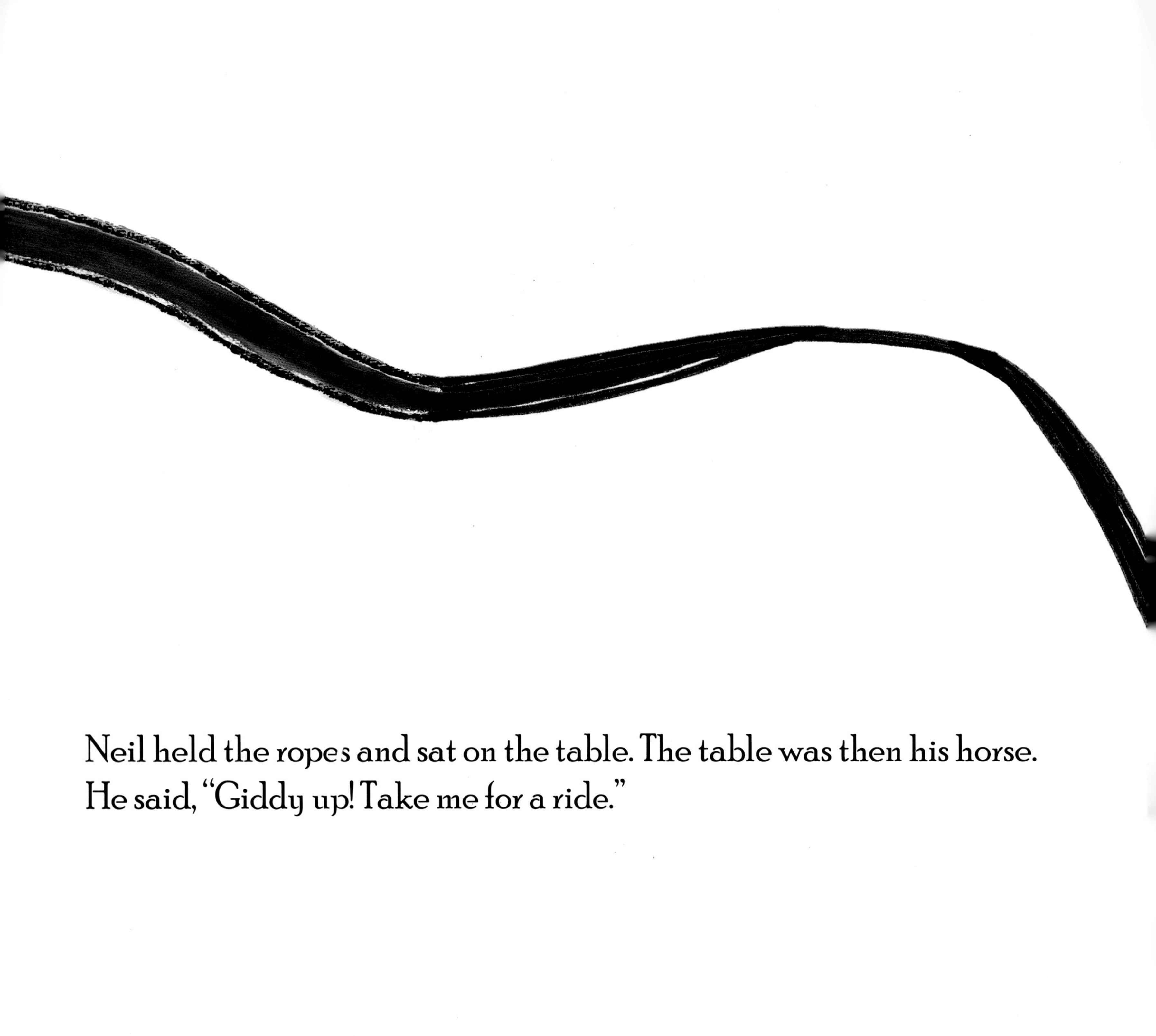

Neil held the ropes and sat on the table. The table was then his horse.
He said, "Giddy up! Take me for a ride."

Neil blew his whistle.

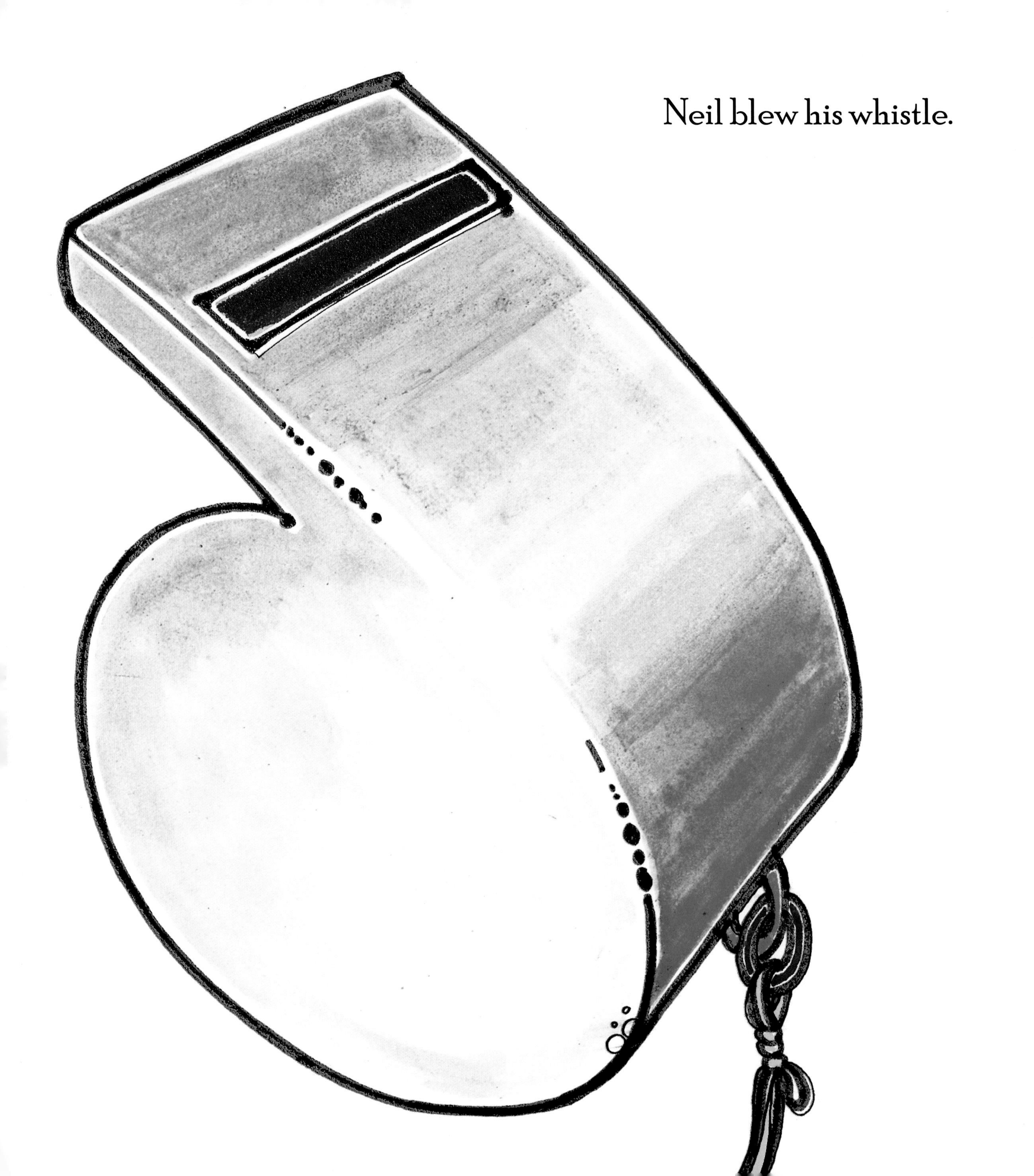

Neil put colored baskets on the table.
There were flowers and candies in
the baskets.

Neil then pushed the table. The table became his push toy.
"Dash...dash!" the table moved slowly. Neil laughed with joy.

Soon, there came his elder sister, Monica.
Monica wore a beautiful frock.
She was taller than Neil.

"Let us play together, Monica," said Neil.
They both sat under the table.

Neil's toys lay around him. He rested in his sister's lap. Monica told him a story.

MY
BED
TIME
BOOK
2

Neil enjoyed listening to the story.
Soon, he felt sleepy.

Neil slept in Monica's arms. What fun it was!

The Parrot

Neera was a little girl. She loved animals.

One day, Neera saw a parrot in a cage.
The parrot looked sad. It was crying.

Neera put a piece of bread in the cage.
The parrot did not eat it.

Neera gave water to the parrot.
The parrot did not drink it.

The parrot screeched and
flapped its wings.

Neera thought, "Oh, the parrot must be missing its mother."

Neera opened the door of the cage.

The parrot flew away. Neera was very happy.

The parrot was also happy to be free again.